little MONKEY

marta altés

MACMILLAN CHILDREN'S BOOKS

Monkey loved living in the jungle.

There were so many things to do
and so many things to see.

To Emily
and all the fearless little monkeys.

Thanks to my editor Emily Ford
and designer Lorna Scobie

First published 2016 by Macmillan Children's Books
This edition published 2018 by Macmillan Children's Books
an imprint of Pan Macmillan
20 New Wharf Road, London N1 9RR
Associated companies throughout the world
www.panmacmillan.com
ISBN: 978-1-5290-0231-7

But every now and then . . .

Ooof!

Things went
a bit wrong.

Monkey had
a little problem.

And the problem
was being little.

Some days everything was out of reach.

Other days it was out of sight.

LOOK!

WOW!

Things were always too deep,

too dangerous

and too difficult
for someone so little.

NO, YOU CAN'T
CLIMB UP HERE.

Monkey was fed up with always missing out.

So one day she made a decision.
A very brave and very BIG decision.

"I will climb to the top of the tallest tree.
The jungle is NOT too big for me,
you'll see!"

It wasn't an easy journey.

Not easy at all.

The river was deep and dangerous.

The path was often difficult.

But Monkey would not give up

and, step by step, she found her way.

Everywhere Monkey looked she noticed little things.

And the little things did amazing things!

"Now it's my turn," she said.

So Monkey
began to count.

"One,

two . . .

threeeeeeeeeee . . . !"

"Who's too
little now?

NOT ME."

Soon Monkey
had reached
the very bottom
of the tallest tree
in the jungle.

"This will be fun,"
she said, and
she began
to climb.

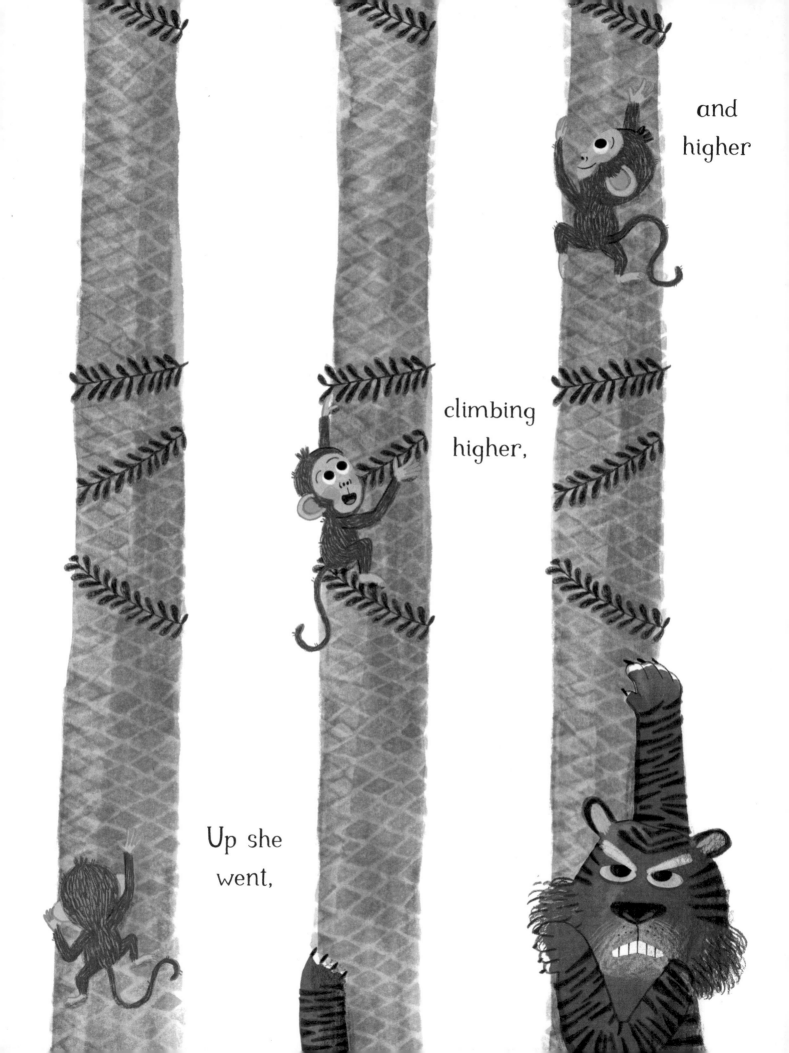

and
higher

climbing
higher,

Up she
went,

. . . right to the very top.

The world below looked
so little and so beautiful!

Finally Monkey could see EVERYTHING!

Including the rest of her troop.

"They look very excited
to see me!"

It must be time to go, thought Monkey,

and she swung down from the tallest tree,

feeling very pleased and very proud.

Monkey did love living in the jungle,

now more than ever before.

"I may be small but I'm very brave," she said.

"And very lucky!"
said the rest of the troop.

Little Monkey knew they were right.
Because the smaller you are, the
larger your adventures can be.

But best of all . . .

the bigger the hugs feel.